Belle Marvel Brain, Thomas Fuller

Quaint Thoughts of an Old-Time Army Chaplain

Belle Marvel Brain, Thomas Fuller

Quaint Thoughts of an Old-Time Army Chaplain

ISBN/EAN: 9783337404482

Printed in Europe, USA, Canada, Australia, Japan

Cover: Foto ©Andreas Hilbeck / pixelio.de

More available books at **www.hansebooks.com**

QUAINT THOUGHTS

OF

AN OLD-TIME ARMY CHAPLAIN

Quaint Thoughts

of

An Old-time Army Chaplain

Being fifty selections from
"Good Thoughts for Bad Times"
/ by
Thomas Fuller, D. D.

Compiled and Arranged by
Belle M. Brain

United Society of Christian Endeavor
Boston and Chicago

TO THE BRAVE AND LOYAL

Soldiers and Sailors of '98,

FIGHTING IN THE CAUSE OF LIBERTY AND HUMANITY,

THESE QUAINT THOUGHTS OF AN

OLD-TIME ARMY CHAPLAIN

ARE INSCRIBED BY

THE COMPILER

———

The soldiers asked of John Baptist (Luke 3: 14, etc.): And what shall we do? Every man ought (not curiously to inquire into the duty of others, but) to attend his own concernments. The Baptist returned: Do violence to no man, neither accuse any falsely; and be content with your wages.

Good counsel to the soldiers of this age. Do violence to no man, plunder no man, accuse no man falsely. Make no men malignants by wrongful information, and be content with your wages. — *Thomas Fuller*.

FOREWORD

––––◆––––

THOMAS FULLER was a chaplain in the British army during the great civil war in England. Born in 1608, and dying in 1661, he lived and wrote in stirring times. A wise and witty preacher of the gospel, a brave and courageous army chaplain, and a writer of acknowledged power, he left a record second to none among those who have entered the sacred calling.

Coleridge said of him: "Next to Shakespeare, I am not certain whether Thomas Fuller, beyond all other writers, does not excite in me the sense and emulation of the marvellous. . . . In all his numerous volumes on so many different subjects, it is scarcely too much to say that you will hardly find a page in which some one sentence out of every three does not deserve to be quoted by itself as a motto or as a maxim."

Gathering his material while on his long and tedious marches with the army, he "wrote and

9

practised that he might eradicate error and implant the loftiest virtues in the heart of man." With so noble an end in view, it is no wonder that God so highly honored and so richly blessed his written words.

During our Civil War, an edition of Fuller's "Good Thoughts for Bad Times" was issued, as being especially appropriate to the unhappy condition of the nation. This book has long been out of print; it has seemed wise, therefore, to issue these selections from it, in the hope that the quaint thoughts and the homely expressions may produce an "arrest of thought in many minds, resulting in the good of souls and the glory of God."

BELLE M. BRAIN.

SPRINGFIELD, OHIO, JUNE 8, 1898.

QUAINT THOUGHTS

OF

AN OLD-TIME ARMY CHAPLAIN

———·———

I.

LORD, I do discover a fallacy, whereby I have
long deceived myself.   Which is this : I have desired
to begin my amendment from my birthday, or from
the first day of the year, or from some eminent fes-
tival, that so my repentance might bear some
remarkable date.   But when those days were come,
I have adjourned my amendment to some other
time.   Thus, whilst I could not agree with myself
when to start, I have almost lost the running of the
race.   I am resolved thus to befool myself no
longer.   I see no day equal to to-day; the instant
time is always the fittest time. . . . Grant, therefore, that to-day I may hear thy voice.   And if this
day be obscure in the calendar, and remarkable in
itself for nothing else, give me to make it memorable in my soul, thereupon, by thy assistance,
beginning the reformation of my life.

II.

Behold, now
is the ac-
cepted time;
behold, now
is the day of
salvation.

LORD, often have I thought with myself, I will sin but this one sin more, and then I will repent of it, and of all the rest of my sins together. So foolish was I, and ignorant. As if I should be more able to pay my debts when I owe more: or as if I should say, I will wound my friend once again, and then I will lovingly shake hands with him; but what if my friend will not shake hands with me? . . . Grant, Lord, at this instant I may break off my badness: otherwise thou mayst justly make the last minute wherein I *do* sin on earth to be the last minute wherein I *shall* sin on earth, and the first wherein thou mightest make me suffer in another place.

III.

Remember
now thy Cre-
ator in the
days of thy
youth, while
the evil days
come not.

LORD, when I am to travel, I never use to provide myself till the very time; partly out of laziness, loath to be troubled till needs I must; partly out of pride, as presuming all necessaries for my journey will wait upon me at the instant. . . . Grant, Lord, that my confessed improvidence in temporal, may make me suspect my providence in spiritual, matters. Solomon saith, Man goeth to his long home. Short preparation will not fit so long a journey. O let me not put it off to the last, but let me

so dispose of myself that, when I am to die, *I may
have nothing to do but to die.*

IV.

LORD, I confess this morning I remembered my
breakfast, but forgot my prayers.   And, as I have
returned no praise, so thou mightst justly have
afforded me no protection.   Yet thou hast carefully
kept me to the middle of this day, entrusted me
with a new debt before I have paid the old score.
It is now noon, too late for a morning, too soon for
an evening, sacrifice.   My corrupt heart prompts
me to put off my prayers till night; but I know it
too well, or, rather, too ill, to trust it.   I fear, if till
night I defer them, at night I shall forget them.
Be pleased, therefore, now to accept them. . . . I
promise hereafter, by thy assistance, to bring forth
fruit in due season.   See how I am ashamed the
sun should shine on me, who now newly start in the
race of my devotions, when he, like a giant, hath
run more than half his course in the heavens.

My voice shalt thou hear in the morning, O Lord; in the morning will I direct my prayer unto thee, and will look up.

V.

SHAMEFUL my sloth, that I have deferred my
night prayer till I am in bed.   This lying along is
an improper posture for piety.   Indeed, there is no
contrivance of our body, but some good man in

O come, let us worship and bow down: let us kneel before the Lord our maker. For he is our God.

Scripture hath hanselled it with prayer. The publican standing, Job sitting, Hezekiah lying on his bed, Elijah with his face between his legs. But of all gestures give me St. Paul's: for this cause I bow my knees to the Father of my Lord Jesus Christ. Knees, when they *may*, then they *must*, be bended. . . . I know, in case of necessity, God would graciously accept my devotion, bound down in a sick dressing; but now, whilst I am in perfect health, it is inexcusable. . . . But may God pardon my idleness this once, I will not again offend in the same kind, by his grace hereafter.

VI.

Be not slothful.

Seek ye out of the book of the Lord, and read.

LORD, I discover an arrant laziness in my soul. For, when I am to read a chapter in the Bible, before I begin it, I look where it endeth. And if it endeth not on the same side, I cannot keep my hands from turning over the leaf, to measure the length thereof on the other side; if it swells to many verses, I begin to grudge. Surely, my heart is not rightly affected. Were I truly hungry after heavenly food, I would not complain of meat. Scourge, Lord, this laziness out of my soul; make the reading of thy word not a penance, but a pleasure unto me; teach me that as amongst many heaps of gold, all being equally pure, that is the best which is the biggest, so I may esteem that chapter in thy word the best that is the longest.

VII.

LORD, the motions of thy Holy Spirit were formerly frequent in my heart; but alas! of late they have been great strangers. It seems they did not like their last entertainment, they are so loath to come again. I fear they were grieved, that either I heard them not attentively, or believed them not faithfully, or practised them not conscionably. If they be pleased to come again, this is all I dare promise, that they do deserve, and I do desire, they should be well used.

Grieve not the holy Spirit of God.

VIII.

LORD, thy servants are now praying in the church, and I am here staying at home, detained by necessary occasions, such as are not of my seeking, but of thy sending; my care could not prevent them, my power could not remove them. Wherefore, though I cannot go to church, there to sit down at table with the rest of thy guests, be pleased, Lord, to send me a dish of their meat hither, and feed my soul with holy thoughts. . . . I fear too many at church have their bodies there and minds at home. Behold, in exchange, my body here .

Open thy mouth wide, and I will fill it.

Blessed are they which do hunger and thirst after righteousness: for they shall be filled.

and heart there. Though I cannot pray *with* them, I pray *for* them. Yea, this comforts me, I am with thy congregation, because I would be with it.

IX.

Be filled with the Spirit; speaking to yourselves in psalms and hymns and spiritual songs, singing and making melody in your heart to the Lord.

LORD, my voice by nature is harsh and untunable, and it is vain to lavish any art to better it. Can my singing of psalms be pleasing to thy ears, which is unpleasant to my own? Yet, though I cannot chant with the nightingale, or chirp with the blackbird, I had rather chatter with the swallow, yea, rather croak with the raven, than to be

Whoso offereth praise glorifieth me.

altogether silent. Hadst thou given me a better voice, I would have praised thee with a better voice. Now what my music wants in sweetness, let it have in sense, singing praises with understanding. Yea, Lord, create in me a new heart (therein to make melody), and I will be contented with my old voice, until in thy due time, being admitted into the choir of heaven, I have another, more harmonious, bestowed upon me.

X.

LORD, I perceive my soul deeply guilty of envy. I had rather thy work were undone than done better by another than myself; had rather that thine enemies were all alive than that I should kill but my thousand, and others their ten thousands of them. . . . Dispossess me, Lord, of this bad spirit, and turn my envy into holy emulation. Let me labor to exceed them in pains who excel me in parts; and, knowing that my sword, in cutting down sin, hath a duller edge, let me strike with greater force; yea, make other men's gifts to be mine, by making me thankful to thee for them. . . . Let me feed and foster and nourish and cherish the graces in others, honoring their persons, praising their parts, and glorifying thy name, who hath given such gifts unto them.

In lowliness of mind, let each esteem other better than themselves. Look not every man on his own things, but every man also on the things of others.

XI.

LORD, I find David making a syllogism, in mood and figure, two propositions he perfected. Ps. 66: 18. If I regard wickedness in my heart, the Lord will not hear me.

Not unto us, O Lord, not unto us, but unto thy name give glory.

19. But verily God hath heard me, he hath attended to the voice of my prayer.

Now I expected that David should have concluded thus: —

Therefore I regard not wickedness in my heart.

But far otherwise he concludes: —

20. Blessed be God, who hath not turned away my prayer, nor his mercy from me.

Thus David hath deceived, but not wronged me. I looked that he should have clapped the crown on his own, but he puts it on God's, head; for I like David's better than Aristotle's syllogisms, that, whatsoever the premises be, I make God's glory the conclusion.

XII.

If we confess our sins, he is faithful and just to forgive us our sins, and to cleanse us from all un-righteous-ness.

LORD, before I commit a sin, it seems to me so shallow, that I may wade through it dry-shod from any guiltiness; but when I have committed it, it often seems so deep that I cannot escape without drowning. Thus I am always in the extremities: either my sins are so small that they need not my repentance, or so great that they cannot obtain thy pardon. Lend me, O Lord, a reed out of thy sanctuary, truly to measure the dimensions of my offences. But O, as thou revealest to me more of my misery, reveal also more of thy mercy. If my badness seem bigger than thy goodness, but one hair's breadth, but one moment, that is room and time enough for me to run to eternal despair.

XIII.

A SAGAMORE, or petty king in Virginia, guessing the greatness of other kings by his own, sent a native hither, who understood English; commanding him to score upon a long cane (given him of purpose to be his register) the number of Englishmen, that hereby his master might know the strength of our nation. Landing at Plymouth, a popular place, he had no leisure to eat, for notching up the men he met. At Exeter the difficulty of his task was increased; coming at last to London (that forest of people) he broke his cane in pieces, perceiving the impossibility of his employment. Some may con·ceive that they can reckon up the sins they commit in one day. Perchance they may make hard shifts to sum up their notorious ill deeds; more difficult it is to score up their wicked words. But O how infinite are their idle thoughts! High time, then, to leave off counting, and cry out with David, Who can tell how oft he offendeth? Lord, cleanse me from my secret sins.

Mine iniquities . . . are more than the hairs of mine head: therefore my heart faileth me. Be pleased, O Lord, to deliver me.

XIV.

ALMOST twenty years since I heard a profane jest, and still remember it. How many pious passages of far later date have I forgotten! It seems my soul is like a filthy pond, wherein fish die soon, and frogs live long. Lord, raze this profane jest out of my memory. Leave not a letter thereof behind, lest my corruption (an apt scholar) guess it out again; and be pleased to write some pious meditation in the place thereof. And grant, Lord, for the time to come (because such bad guests are easier kept out), that I may be careful not to admit what I find so difficult to expel.

Wash me thoroughly from mine iniquity, and cleanse me from my sin.

XV.

In that day there shall be a fountain opened to the house of David, and to the inhabitants of Jerusalem for sin and for uncleanness.

THE poets fable that this was one of the labors imposed on Hercules: to make clean the Augean stable, or stall, rather. For therein, they said, were kept three thousand kine, and it had not been cleansed for thirty years together. But Hercules, by letting the river Alpheus into it, did with ease what was before conceived impossible. This stall is the pure emblem of my impure soul, which hath been defiled with millions of sins for more than thirty years together. O that I might, by a lively faith and unfeigned repentance, let the stream of that fountain into my soul, which is opened for Judah and Jerusalem. It is impossible by all my pains to purge out my uncleanness; which is quickly done by the rivulet of the blood of my Saviour.

XVI.

Let us lift up our heart with our hands unto God in the heavens.

LORD, this day I disputed with myself whether or no I had said my prayers this morning, and I could not call to mind any remarkable passage whence I could certainly conclude that I had offered my prayers unto thee. Frozen affections, which left no spark of remembrance behind them! Yet at last I hardly recovered one token whence I was assured that I had said my prayers. It seems I had said them, and only *said* them, rather *by* heart than *with* my heart. Can I hope that thou wouldst remember my prayers, when I had almost forgotten that I had prayed? Or, rather, have I not cause to fear that thou rememberest my prayers too well, to punish the coldness and badness of them? Alas! are not devotions, thus done, in effect left undone? Well Jacob advised his sons, at their second going into Egypt, Take double money in your hand; peradventure it was an oversight. So, Lord, I come with my second morning sacrifice; be pleased to accept it, which I desire and endeavor to present with a little better devotion than I did the former.

XVII.

LORD, how come wicked thoughts to perplex me in my prayers, when I desire and endeavor only to attend thy service? Now I perceive the cause thereof; at other times I have willingly entertained them, and now they entertain themselves against my will. I acknowledge thy justice, that what formerly I have invited, now I cannot expel. Give me hereafter always to bolt out such ill guests. The best way to be rid of such bad thoughts in my prayers is not to receive them out of my prayers.

Keep thy heart with all diligence; for out of it are the issues of life.

XVIII.

Search me,
O God, and
know my
heart : try
me, and
know my
thoughts ;
and see if
there be any
wicked way
in me, and
lead me in
the way ever-
lasting.

FINDING a bad thought in my heart, I disputed in myself the cause thereof, whether it proceeded from the devil or my own corruption, examining it by those signs divines in this case recommended.

1. Whether it came in incoherently, or by dependence on some object presented to my senses.

2. Whether the thought was at full age at the first instant, or, infant-like, grew greater by degrees.

3. Whether out or in the road of my natural inclinations.

But hath not this inquiry more of curiosity than religion ? Hereafter, derive not the pedigree, but make the mittimus of such malefactors. Suppose a confederacy betwixt thieves without and false servants within, to assault and wound the master of a family; thus wounded, would he discuss from which of them his hurts proceeded ? No, surely; but speedily send for a surgeon before he bleed to death. I will no more put it to the question, whence my bad thoughts come, but whither I shall send them, lest this curious controversy betray me into a consent unto them.

XIX.

LORD, let thy Holy Spirit be pleased, not only to stand before the door and knock, but also to come in. If I do not open the door, it were too unreasonable to request such a miracle to come in when the doors were shut, as thou didst to the apostles. Yet let me humbly beg of thee that thou wouldst make the iron gate of my heart open of its own accord. Then let thy Spirit be pleased to sup in my heart; I have given him an invitation, and I hope I shall give him room. But, O thou that sendest the guest, send the meat also; and if I be so unmannerly as not to make the Holy Spirit welcome, O let thy effectual grace make me to make him welcome.

Behold, I stand at the door and knock: if any man hear my voice, and open the door, I will come in to him, and will sup with him, and he with me.

XX.

LORD, this morning I read a chapter in the Bible, and therein observed a memorable passage, whereof I never took notice before. Why now, and not sooner, did I see it? Formerly my eyes were as open, and the letters as legible. Is there not a thin veil laid over thy word, which is more rarefied by reading, and at last wholly worn away? . . . I see the oil of thy word will never leave increasing whilst any bring an empty barrel. The Old Testament will still be a New Testament to him who comes with a fresh desire of information.

Open thou mine eyes that I may behold wondrous things out of thy law.

XXI.

The son shall not bear the iniquity of the father, neither shall the father bear the iniquity of the son; the righteousness of the righteous shall be upon him, and the wickedness of the wicked shall be upon him.

LORD, I find the genealogy of my Saviour strangely checkered with four remarkable changes in four immediate generations.

1. Roboam begat Abia; that is, a bad father begat a bad son.

2. Abia begat Asa; that is, a bad father, a good son.

3. Asa begat Josaphat; that is, a good father, a good son.

4. Josaphat begat Joram; that is, a good father, a bad son.

I see, Lord, from hence, that my father's piety cannot be entailed; that is bad news for me. But I see also that actual impiety is not always hereditary; that is good news for my son.

XXII.

Now no chastening for the present seemeth to be joyous, but grievous; nevertheless afterward it yieldeth the peaceable fruit of righteousness unto them which are exercised thereby.

LORD, what faults I correct in my son, I commit myself: I beat him for dabbling in the dirt, whilst my own soul doth wallow in sin; I beat him for crying to cut his own meat, yet am not, myself, contented with that state thy providence hath carved unto me; I beat him for crying when he is to go to sleep, and yet I fear I myself shall cry when thou callest me to sleep with my fathers. Alas! I am more childish than my child, and what I inflict on him, I justly deserve to receive from thee, only here is the difference: I pray and desire that my correction on my child may do him good; it is in thy power, Lord, to effect that thy correction on me shall do me good.

XXIII.

I saw two children fighting together on the street. The father of one, passing by, fetched his son away and corrected him; the other lad was left without any check, though both were equally faulty in the fray. I was half offended that, being guilty alike, they were not punished alike; but the parent would only meddle with him over whom he had an undoubted dominion, to whom he bare an unfeigned affection.

My son, despise not the chastening of the Lord; neither be weary of his correction: for whom the Lord loveth he correcteth; even as a father the son in whom he delighteth.

The wicked sin, the godly smart most in this world. God singleth out his own sons, and beateth them by themselves; whom he loveth he chasteneth, whilst the ungodly, preserved from affliction, are reserved for destruction, it being needless that their hair should be shaved with a hired razor, whose heads are intended for the axe of divine justice.

XXIV.

Lord, many temporal matters which I have desired thou hast denied me; it vexed me for the

We know that all things work together for good to them that love God, to them who are the called according to his purpose.

present that I wanted my will; since, considering in cold blood, I plainly perceive, had that which I desired been done, I had been undone! Yea, what thou gavest me, instead of those things which I wished, though less toothsome to me, were more wholesome for me. Forgive, I pray, my former anger, and now accept my humble thanks. Lord, grant me one suit, which is this: deny me all suits which are bad for me; when I petition for what is unfitting, O let the King of heaven make use of his negative voice. Rather let me fast than have quails given with intent that I should be choked in eating them.

XXV.

Blessed be the Lord, who daily loadeth us with benefits.

AMONGST other arguments enforcing the necessity of daily prayer, this not the least, that Christ enjoins us to petition for daily bread. New bread we know is best; and in a spiritual sense our bread,

Evening, and morning, and at noon, will I pray, and cry aloud; and he shall hear my voice.

though in itself as stale and mouldy as that of the Gibeonites, is every day new, because a new and hot blessing, as I might say, is daily begged, and bestowed of God upon it. Manna must be daily gathered, and not provisionally hoarded up. God expects that men every day address themselves unto him, by petitioning him for sustenance.

How contrary is this to the common practice of many! As camels in sandy countries are said to drink but once in seven days, and then *in præsens, præteritum, et futurum,* for time past, present, and to come, so many fumble this, last, and next week's devotion all in a prayer. Yea, some defer all their praying till the last day.

XXVI.

PERCHANCE my prayer may extend to a quarter of an hour, when poured out at large. But some days I begrudge this time as too much, and omit the preface of my prayer, with some passages conceived less material, and run two or three petitions into one, so contracting them to half a quarter of an hour.

What, could ye not watch with me one hour? Watch and pray, that ye enter not into temptation.

Not long after, this also seems too long ; I decontract and abridge the abridgment of my prayers, yea (be it confessed to my shame and sorrow, that hereafter I may amend it), too often I shrink my prayers to a minute, to a moment, to a Lord have mercy upon me !

XXVII.

EJACULATIONS are short prayers darted up to God on emergent occasions. Their principal use is against the fiery darts of the devil. Our adversary injects (*how* he doth it God knows, *that* he doth it we know) bad motions into our hearts, and that we

Above all, taking the shield of faith, wherewith ye shall be able to quench all the fiery darts of the wicked.

may be as nimble with our antidotes as he with his poisons, such short prayers are proper and necessary. In barred havens, so choked up with the envious sands that great ships, drawing many feet of water, cannot come near, lighter and lesser pinnaces may freely and safely arrive. When we are timebound, place-bound, or person-bound, so that we cannot compose ourselves to make a large solemn prayer, this is the right instant for ejaculations, whether orally uttered, or only poured forth inwardly in the heart.

XXVIII.

Pray without ceasing. Men ought always to pray, and not to faint.

EJACULATORY prayers give liberty of callings, so that at the same instant one may follow his proper vocation. The husbandman may dart forth an ejaculation, and not make a balk the more. The seaman nevertheless steer his ship right in the darkest night. Yea, the soldier at the same time may shoot out his prayer to God and aim his pistol at the enemy, the one better hitting the mark for the other. Ejaculations bind not men to any bodily observances, only busy the spiritual half, which maketh them consistent with the prosecution of any other employment.

XXIX.

COMING hastily into a chamber, I had almost thrown down a crystal hour-glass. Fear lest I had, made me grieve as if I had broken it. But alas! how much precious time have I cast away without any regret! The hour-glass was but crystal, while each hour is a pearl; that but like to be broken, this lost outright; that but casually, this done wilfully. A better hour-glass might be bought; but time, lost once, is lost forever. Thus we grieve more for toys than for treasure. Lord, give me an hourglass, not to be by me, but to be in me. Teach me to number my days. An hour-glass to turn me, that I may apply my heart unto wisdom.

See then that ye walk circumspectly, not as fools, but as wise, redeeming the time, because the days are evil.

XXX.

WE read that the nails in the holy of holies (2 Chronicles 3 : 8 and 9) were of fine gold. Hence ariseth a question how such nails could be useful, pure gold being so flexible that a nail made thereof will bow, and not drive.

In quietness and in confidence shall be your strength.

Now, I was present at the debate thereof, betwixt the best working goldsmiths in London, where, among many ingenious answers, this carried away the credit for the greatest probability thereof; viz., that they were screw-nails, which had holes prepared for their reception, and so were wound in by degrees.

God's work must not be done lazily, but leisurely: haste maketh waste in this kind. In reformations of great importance, the violent driving in of the nail will either break the head, or bow the point thereof, or rive and split that which should be fastened therewith. That may insensibly be screwed, which cannot suddenly be knocked into people. Fair and softly goeth far; but alas! we have too many fiery spirits, who, with Jehu, drive on so furiously they will overturn all in church and state, if their fierceness be not seasonably retrenched.

XXXI.

Therefore, behold, I will hedge up thy way with thorns.

WHEN I go speedily in any action, Lord, give me to call my soul to an account. It is a shrewd suspicion that my bowl runs down-hill, because it runs so fast. And, Lord, if I go in an unlawful way, start some rubs to stop me, let my foot slip or stumble. And give me the grace to understand the language of the lets [1] thou throwest in my way. Thou hast promised, I will hedge up thy way. Lord, be pleased to make the hedge high enough and thick enough, that if I be so mad as to adventure to climb over it, I may not only soundly rake my clothes, but rend my flesh; yea, let me rather be caught, and stick in the hedge, than, breaking in through it, fall on the other side into the deep ditch of eternal damnation.

[1] Hindrances.

XXXII.

LORD, this day casually I am fallen into a bad company, and know not how I came hither, or how to get hence. Sure I am, not my improvidence hath run me, but thy providence hath led me, into this danger. I was not wandering in any base by-path, but walking in the highway of my vocation; wherefore, Lord, thou that callest me hither, keep me here. Stop their mouths, that they speak no blasphemy, or stop my ears, that I hear none; or open my mouth soberly to reprove what I hear. Give me to guard myself; but, Lord, guard my guarding of myself. Let not the smoke of their badness put out mine eyes, but the shining of my innocency lighten theirs. Let me give physic to them, and not take infection from them. Yea, make me the better for their badness.

Blessed is the man that endureth temptation: for when he is tried he shall receive the crown of life, which the Lord hath promised to them that love him.

XXXIII.

LORD, I trust thou hast pardoned the bad examples I have set before others; be pleased also to pardon me the sins which they have committed by my bad examples. (It is best manners in thy court to heap requests upon requests.) If thou hast forgiven my sins, the children of my corrupt nature, forgive me my grandchildren also. Let not the transcripts remain since thou hast blotted out the original.

As far as the east is from the west, so far hath he removed our transgressions from us.

XXXIV.

I am not ashamed of the gospel of Christ: for it is the power of God unto salvation to every one that believeth.

A PERSON of great quality was pleased to lodge a night in my house. I durst not invite him to my family prayer; and therefore, for that time, omitted it; thereby making a breach in a good custom, and giving Satan advantage to assault it. Yea, the loosening of such a link might have endangered the scattering of the chain.

Bold bashfulness, which durst offend God whilst it did fear man. Especially considering, that, though my guest was never so high, yet by the laws of hospitality I was above him whilst he was under my roof.

Hereafter, whosoever cometh within the doors shall be requested to come within the discipline of my house; if accepting my homely diet, he will not refuse my home devotion; and sitting by my table, will be entreated to kneel down by it.

XXXV.

Yet the Lord will command his loving-kindness in the daytime, and in the night his song shall be with me, and my

DEATH in Scripture is compared to sleep. Well then may my night prayer be resembled to making my will. I will be careful not to die intestate; as also not to defer my will-making till I am not *compos mentis*, till the lethargy of drowsiness seize upon me. . . . Night was made for man to rest in. But when I cannot sleep, may I entertain my waking with good thoughts. Not to use them as opium, to invite my corrupt nature to slumber, but to bolt out bad thoughts, which otherwise would possess my soul.

prayer unto the God of my life.

XXXVI.

LORD, be pleased to shake my clay cottage before thou throwest it down. May it totter awhile before it doth tumble. Let me be summoned before I am surprised. Deliver me from sudden death. Not from sudden death in respect of itself, for I care not how short my passage be, so it be safe. Never any weary traveller complained that he came too soon to his journey's end. But let it not be sudden in respect of me. Make me always ready to receive death. Thus no guest comes unawares to him who keeps a constant table.

Take ye heed, watch and pray; for ye know not when the time is. Be ye therefore ready also.

XXXVII.

LORD, how near was I to danger, yet escaped! I was upon the brink of the brink of it, yet fell not in; they are well kept who are kept by thee. Excellent archer! Thou didst hit thy mark in missing it, as meaning to fright, not hurt me. Let me not now be such a fool as to pay my thanks to blind Fortune

Thou, Lord, only makest me to dwell in safety. My times are in thy hand.

for a favor which the eye of Providence hath bestowed upon me. Rather let the narrowness of my escape make my thankfulness to thy goodness the larger, lest my ingratitude justly cause that, whereas this arrow but hit my hat, the next pierce my head.

XXXVIII.

When thou vowest a vow unto God, defer not to pay it; for he hath no pleasure in fools; pay that which thou hast vowed.

LORD, I read how Jacob (then only accompanied with his staff) vowed at Bethel that, if thou gavest him but bread and raiment, he would make that place thy house. After his return, the condition on thy side was over-performed, but the obligation on his part wholly neglected : for when thou hadst made his staff to swell, and to break into two bands, he, after his return, turned purchaser, bought a field in Shalem, intending there to set up his rest. But thou wert pleased to be his remembrancer in a new vision, and to spur him afresh, who tired in his promise. Arise, go to Bethel, and make there an altar, etc. Lord, if rich Jacob forgot what poor Jacob did promise, no wonder if I be bountiful to offer thee in my affliction what I am niggardly to perform in my prosperity. But O, take not advantage of the forfeitures, but be pleased to demand payment once again. Pinch me into the remembrance of my promise, that so I may re-enforce my old vows with new resolutions.

XXXIX.

THE Amalekite who brought tidings to David (2 Samuel 1) began with truth, rightly reporting the overthrow of the Israelites; cheaters must get some credit before they can cozen, and all falsehood, if not founded in some truth, would not be fixed in any belief.

Lying lips are abomination to the Lord. Wherefore putting away lying, speak every man truth with his neighbor.

But, proceeding, he told six lies successively:

1. That Saul called him.
2. That he came at his call.
3. That Saul demanded who he was.
4. That he returned his answer.
5. That Saul commanded to kill him.
6. That he killed him accordingly.

A wilful falsehood told is a cripple not able to stand by itself, without some to support it; it is easy to tell a lie, hard to tell but one lie. Lord, if I be so unhappy as to relate a falsehood, give me to recall it, or repent of it.

XL.

LORD, wise Agur made it his wish, Give me not poverty lest I steal, and take the name of my God in vain. He saith not, Lest I steal and be caught in the manner, and then be stocked, or whipped, or branded, or forced to fourfold restitution, or put

Seeing they crucify the Son of God afresh, and put him to an open shame.

to any other shameful or painful punishment. But
he saith, Lest I steal, and take the name of my
God in vain; that is, Lest, professing to serve
thee, I confute a good profession with a bad con-
versation. Thus thy children count sin to be the
greatest smart in sin, as being more sensible of
the wound they therein give to the glory of God
than of all the stripes man may lay upon them for
punishment.

XLI.

Provide
things honest
in the sight
of all men.
Thou shalt
not defraud
thy neigh-
bor, neither
rob him: the
wages of him
that is hired
shall not
abide with
thee all night
until the
morning.

I CARE not how small my means be, so they be
my means; I mean my own without any injury
to others. What is truly gotten may be comfort-
ably kept. What is otherwise may be possessed,
but not enjoyed.

Upon the question, What is the worst bread
which is eaten? one answered, in respect of the
coarseness thereof, Bread made of beans. Another said, Bread made of acorns. But the third
hit the truth, who said, Bread taken out of other
men's mouths, who are the true proprietaries
thereof. Such bread may be sweet in the mouth
to taste, but is not wholesome in the stomach to
digest. . . . Lord, grant that though my means be
never so small, they may be my means, not wrong-
fully detained from others having a truer title to
them.

XLII.

THIS seeming paradox will, on examination, prove a real truth; viz., that though Job lost his seven thousand sheep consumed by fire of God, Job 1 : 16 (understand it, by his permission, and Satan's immission), yet he still kept the wool of many of them.

For Job, in the vindication of his integrity (not to praise, but to purge, himself), doth relate how the loins of the poor blessed him, being warmed with the fleece of his sheep (Job 31 : 20). So much of his wool (in the cloth made thereof) he secured in a safe hand, lending it to God (in poor people), Prov. 19 : 17, as the best of debtors, being most able and willing to repay it.

Such as have been plundered of their estates in these wars may content and comfort themselves with this consideration, that so long as they enjoyed plenty, they freely parted with a proportion thereof to the relief of the poor; what they gave, that they have; it still remaineth theirs, and is safely laid up for them in a place where rust and moth do not corrupt, nor thieves break through and steal.

Charge them that are rich in this world . . . that they do good, that they be rich in good works, ready to distribute, willing to communicate; laying up in store for themselves a good foundation against the time to come.

XLIII.

WELL fare their hearts who will not only wear out their shoes, but also their feet, in God's service, and yet gain not a shoe-latchet thereby.

Do good, and lend, hoping for nothing again; and your reward shall be great, and ye shall be the children of the Highest.

When our Saviour drove the sheep and oxen out of the temple, he did not drive them into his own pasture, nor swept the coin into his own pockets when he overturned the tables of the money-changers. But we have in our days many who are forward to offer to God such zeal which not only cost them nothing, but wherewith they have gained great estates.

XLIV.

It is the Lord; let him do what seemeth him good.

LORD, I read at the transfiguration that Peter, James, and John were admitted to behold Christ, but Andrew was excluded. So again, at the reviving of the daughter of the ruler of the synagogue, these three were let in, and Andrew was shut out. Lastly, in the agony, the aforesaid three were called to be witnesses thereof, and still Andrew left behind. Yet he was Peter's brother, and a good man, and an apostle. Why did not Christ take the two pair of brothers? Was it not a pity to part them? But methinks I seem more offended thereat than Andrew himself was, whom I find to express no discontent, being pleased to be accounted a loyal subject for the general, though he was no favorite in these particulars. Give me to be pleased in myself, and thankful to thee for what I am, though I be not equal to others in personal perfections.

For such peculiar privileges are courtesies from thee when given, and no injuries to us when denied.

XLV.

I HAVE a great friend whom I endeavor and desire to please, but hitherto all in vain : the more I seek, the farther off I am from finding his favor. Whence comes this? Are not my applications to man more frequent than my addresses to my Maker ? Do I not love his smiles more than I fear Heaven's frowns? I confess, to my shame, that sometimes his anger hath grieved me more than my sins. Hereafter by thy assistance, I will labor to approve my ways in God's presence; so shall I either have, or not need, his friendship, and either please him with more ease, or displease him with less danger.

Not as pleasing men, but God, which trieth our hearts.

XLVI.

THE mystery of annealing glass; that is, baking it so that the color may go clean through it, is now by some casualty quite lost in England, if not in Europe. Break a piece of glass painted some four hundred years since, and it will be found as red in the middle as in the outsides ; the color is not only *on* it, but in it, and *through* it. Whereas, now all art can perform is only to fix the red on one side of the glass.

Let us not love in word, neither in tongue ; but in deed and in truth. For the Lord seeth not as man seeth ; for man looketh on the outward appearance, but the Lord looketh on the heart.

I suspect a much more important mystery is much

lost in our age; viz., the transmitting of piety clean through the heart, that a man become inside and outside alike. O the sincerity of the ancient patriarchs, inspired prophets, holy apostles, patient martyrs, and pious fathers of the primitive church, whereas only outside sanctity is too usual in our age. Happy the man on whose monument that character of Asa (1 Kings 15 : 14) may be truly inscribed for his epitaph : Here lieth the man whose heart was perfect with the Lord all his days. Heart perfect, O finest of wares ! All his days, O the largest of measures !

XLVII.

Whosoever drinketh of the water that I shall give him shall never thirst; but the water that I shall give him shall be in him a well of water, springing up into everlasting life.

THE Venetians showed the treasure of their state, being in many great coffers full of gold and silver, to the Spanish ambassador. But the ambassador, peeking under the bottom of those coffers, demanded whether that their treasure did daily grow, and had a root ; for such, saith he, my master's treasure hath, meaning both his Indies. Many men have attained to a great height of piety, to be very abundant and rich therein. But all theirs is but a cistern, not a fountain of grace ; only God's goodness hath a spring of itself in itself.

XLVIII.

LORD, the apostle saith to the Corinthians, God will not suffer you to be tempted above what you are able. But how comes he to contradict himself, by his own confession, in his next epistle? where, speaking of his own sickness, he saith, We were pressed out of measure, above strength. Perchance this will be expounded by propounding another riddle of the same apostle's, who, praising Abraham, saith that against hope he believed in hope. That is, against carnal hope, he believed in spiritual hope. So the same wedge will serve to cleave the former difficulty. Paul was pressed above his human, but not above his heavenly, strength. Grant, Lord, that I may not mangle and dismember thy word, but study it entirely, comparing one place with another. For diamonds can only cut diamonds, and no such comments on the Scripture as the Scripture.

My grace is sufficient for thee; for my strength is made perfect in weakness.

XLIX.

WHEN Herod had beheaded John the Baptist, some might expect that his disciples would have done some great matter in revenge of their master's death. But see how they behave themselves. And his disciples came and took up the body and buried it, and went and told Jesus. And was this all? and what was all this? Alas, poor men, it was some solace to their sorrowful souls that they might lament their loss to a fast friend, who, though for the present unable to help, was willing to pity them.

The apostles gathered themselves together unto Jesus, and told him all things.

Trust in him at all times; ye people, pour out your heart before him; God is a refuge for us.

Hast thou thy body unjustly imprisoned, or thy goods violently detained, or thy credit causelessly defamed? I have a design whereby thou shalt revenge thyself, even go and tell Jesus. Make to him a plain and true report of the manner and measure of thy sufferings; especially there being a great difference betwixt Jesus then clouded in the flesh, and Jesus now shining in glory, having now as much pity, and more power, to redress thy grievances. I know it is counted but a cowardly trick for boys, when beaten but by their equals, to cry that they will tell their father. But, during the present necessity, it is both the best wisdom and valor, even to complain to thy Father in heaven, who will take thy case into his serious consideration.

L.

He shall cover thee with his feathers, and under his wings shalt thou trust; his truth shall be thy shield and buckler.

GOD is said to have brought the Israelites out of Egypt on eagles' wings. Now eagles, when removing their young ones, have a different posture from other fowl, proper to themselves (fit it is that there should be a distinction between sovereign and subjects), carrying their prey in their talons, but young ones on their backs, so interposing their whole bodies betwixt them and harm. The old eagle's body is the young eagle's shield, and must be shot through before her young ones can be hurt.

Thus God, in saving the Jews, put himself betwixt them and danger. Surely God, so loving under the law, is no less gracious in the gospel; our souls are better secured, not only above his wings, but in his body; your life is hid with Christ in God. No fear then of harm; God first must be pierced before we can be prejudiced.